POCKET PIRATES

THE GREAT FLYTRAP DISASTER

3

CHRIS MOULD

ALADDIN
New York London Toronto Sydney New Delhi

ALADDIN
An imprint of Simon & Schuster Children's Publishing Division
1230 Avenue of the Americas, New York, New York 10020
This Aladdin paperback edition February 2019

Originally published in Great Britain by Hodder Children's Books
Published under license from the British publisher
Hodder & Stoughton Limited on behalf of its publishing imprint
Hodder Children's Books, a division of Hachette Children's Group
Also available in an Aladdin hardcover edition.

Cover designed by Karin Paprocki
Interior designed by Michael Rosamilia
The illustrations for this book were rendered in pen and ink.
The text of this book was set in New Century Schoolbook.
Manufactured in the United States of America 0119 OFF
2 4 6 8 10 9 7 5 3 1
Library of Congress Control Number 2018958253
ISBN 978-1-4814-9121-1 (hc)
ISBN 978-1-4814-9120-4 (pbk)
ISBN 978-1-4814-9122-8 (eBook)

FOR J.J. & JOSH

BUTTON
LILY
THE BASEBOARD MICE

CAPTAIN CRABSTICKS
OLD UNCLE NOGGIN
JONES
MR. DREGBY

CONTENTS

The Old Junk Shop

At the end of the street is an old junk shop. It's gloomy and shabby and nothing ever happens there. At least, that's what most people think. . . .

Among the odds and ends and things of no use, a dusty ship in a bottle sits gathering cobwebs on a shelf. But when the world isn't watching, a tiny pirate crew comes out to explore.

And when you're smaller than a teacup, a junk shop can be a pretty dangerous place. . . .

Buzz Bombs

Button awoke to a loud noise. He couldn't quite work out what it was, so he hopped down from his hammock. "What on earth is happening?" he asked, as he climbed through the glass neck of the bottle to see what all the commotion was.

There is no such thing as a normal day

on the shelf. When you are smaller than a pepper shaker, you are often faced with some kind of wild adventure. And while the Pocket Pirates had been enjoying a good long summer, the blazing sun had brought all sorts of problems. As Captain Crabsticks had just discovered, even a gentle morning's walk past the old books to the candlestick could be filled with deadly terror.

Button was deafened by a terrible buzzing. Rubbing his tired eyes, he caught sight of his captain. Sword drawn, Captain Crabsticks was battling a fly that was as big as a Labrador would be to me and you.

Bzzzzzzzzzzz it droned, as it darted around him. The Captain thrust his sword

in its direction. The fly was fast, but the sword hand of the Captain was a good match for it.

"Away, you blighter. Go on, old chap, shoo." He darted around, darning needle in hand.

Button watched, enjoying the entertainment. "Lily, over here!" he shouted. "I've not seen a good pirate versus insect swordfight for a while." His shipmate and best friend, Lily, appeared out of the bottle to join him. The flies and wasps had been driving them crazy and hopefully the Captain's steel blade would teach them a lesson.

"How exciting," gasped Lily.

Swoosh. One final swash and buckle of the sword sent the giant fly swooping across the back of the shelf, but what happened next was not what they'd expected. By now Uncle Noggin had joined them and the crew stood together watching as the fly crashed straight into a huge spiderweb.

"Oh, poor old thing," said the Captain. "I only meant to scare him off."

The crew stood together, looking up at the web. It had always been tucked in the corner, but recently seemed to be growing at an alarming rate. Mr. Dregby, the house spider, had been feasting on all the flies which had arrived with the hot weather.

The four Pocket Pirates watched the

poor fly struggle in the sticky silk. Then the spider himself appeared, dancing along the thread to take a look at his prize.

"Well, well, well. Thank you so much, Captain. How VERY kind of you to deliver breakfast. To be perfectly honest I'm still full from my last meal, but I'm sure he'll save for later."

And with that he darted along the thread, back into the corner.

"That spider is getting far too big for his boots," said Button. "And look at the size of that web."

"It's getting closer," grumbled Uncle Noggin. "It'll swallow us all up if we're not careful."

“Don’t worry,” said Lily. “There’s not much chance of him swallowing *you* whole.”

"Ooooh, how rude," said Uncle Noggin, giving her a wink and patting his round belly.

They could still see Mr. Dregby's large hairy legs. And when Button looked a little closer, he could spy his six eyes still watching them keenly.

"I think Mr. Dregby's grown too," said Lily.

"I wouldn't be surprised," said Uncle Noggin. "His web is like an all-you-can-eat buffet at the moment."

"Well, at least it's keeping his belly full," Button pointed out. "I hate it when he looks at me with hungry eyes. It makes me nervous."

Bzzzzzzzzzz. Just then another fly swooped by.

"Away, you blustering buzz bomb," cried the Captain, swinging his sword back into action. "That's enough swash-buckling for now. I suggest we all get on board and think about breakfast."

As they returned to the ship, some-thing pattered on the glass bottle above them. Button climbed the mast and perched inside the crow's nest. It was Mr. Dregby, dangling from a strand of web and dropping on to the bottle, his six eyes peering in at them spookily.

"He's never come this close before," Button shouted down to the crew. "I don't

like it. We're going to have to deal with him, good and proper."

"Haul in the cork!" ordered the Captain. The crew gathered on deck and Button and Lily turned the handle sticking out of the cotton reel. As the thread wound its way in, the cork pulled into place, blocking the entrance to the bottle.

"Good work, team. We don't want unwanted guests at the table! Now, I seem to think we have a chunk of boiled egg and a morsel of sausage to split up."

"Sounds good," said Button, his tummy rumbling. "Pirate breakfast is the best meal of the day. Coming right up, Captain."

“What is the Captain reading?” asked Lily, watching him from her vantage point on the ship’s deck. He was lying across the pages of a large book at the back of the shelf. As he read he used his sword to underline the words, mumbling to himself.

"Something about the common house spider," answered Button, who seemed to be spending most of the day looking out through the telescope from the crow's nest. "I think it was all that kerfuffle with Mr. Dregby. Got him thinking about things eight-legged."

Just then Button spotted Mr. Tooey, the junk shop owner. He was walking down the corridor into the main part of the shop, carrying something heavy. Button took hold of the snail shell that was tied to the mast and blew into it, making a loud, hornlike noise. When the crew heard that sound they knew to act quickly. Jones, the ship's cat,

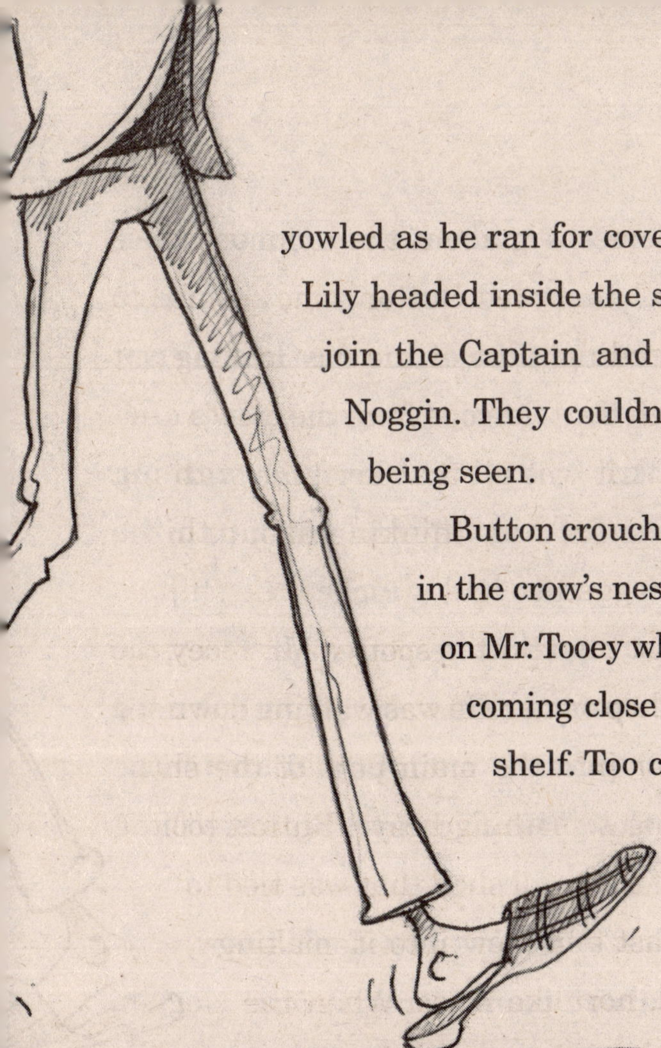

yowled as he ran for cover, and Lily headed inside the ship to join the Captain and Uncle Noggin. They couldn't risk being seen.

Button crouched low in the crow's nest, eyes on Mr. Tooey who was coming close to the shelf. Too close.

It always made them nervous when he was near: even the simplest move could change their lives drastically. They lived in fear of a spring cleaning. One time Mr. Tooey had moved everything onto the floor to tidy the shelf, and the baseboard mice had attacked the ship.

And what was he carrying?

"It's some kind of plant," hissed Button, passing on information to the crew below. "But I've never seen anything like it."

"That's because you don't know anything about plants," said Uncle Noggin. "Here, let me have a look." He edged his head out of the ship so he could see.

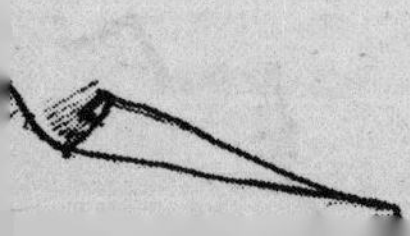

Lily rolled her eyes at him. "What is it then, clever clogs?"

"Aha . . . err, um, OH, I don't know!" muttered Uncle Noggin. "I ain't never seen anything like it either."

Button kept his eye glued to the spyglass.

Mr. Tooey shoved the plant around on the end of the shelf, finding just the right place for it, then he poured a drop of water into the bottom of the pot while his dog fussed around his feet. "There . . . that should help," he murmured.

He tottered off into the kitchen, talking to the dog as he went. "Come on then, old boy, let's get you something to eat."

"That should help?" repeated Button. "What does he mean?"

But no one could answer.

When they were sure he had gone, the Captain gave orders for the cork to be pushed out of the bottle neck and they went outside to look at the curious piece of greenery that had just been delivered.

In the excitement of its arrival, they had forgotten about Mr. Dregby.

And now they gazed in wonder at the towering green monster above them. What was it?

"By Jove, I've nevcr seen anything QUITE like that," said the Captain. "Looks like something tropical."

"Might be something we can eat!" said Uncle Noggin. "Looks like it has some kind of fruit on it."

Bzzzzzzzzz. From the distance, the droning sound of houseflies was approaching. This time there were three of them. The Captain drew his sword and Button grabbed the broken paintbrush that he used to sweep the deck.

Bzzzzzzzz. The noise grew louder. The winged horrors swooped down at the buccaneers. Jones meowed loudly and Lily climbed up the candlestick and

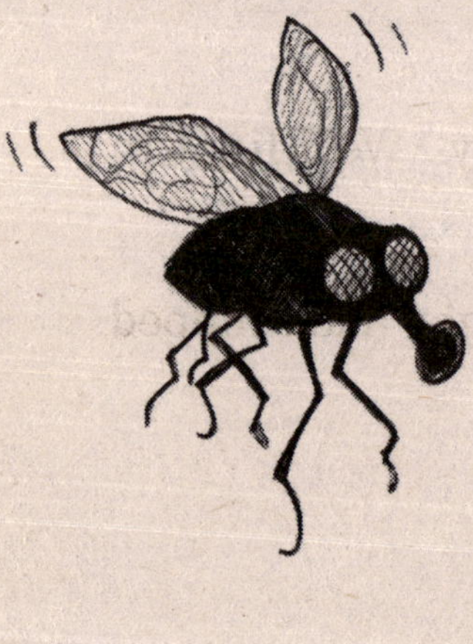

waved the pirate flag at them. "Shoo, shoo."

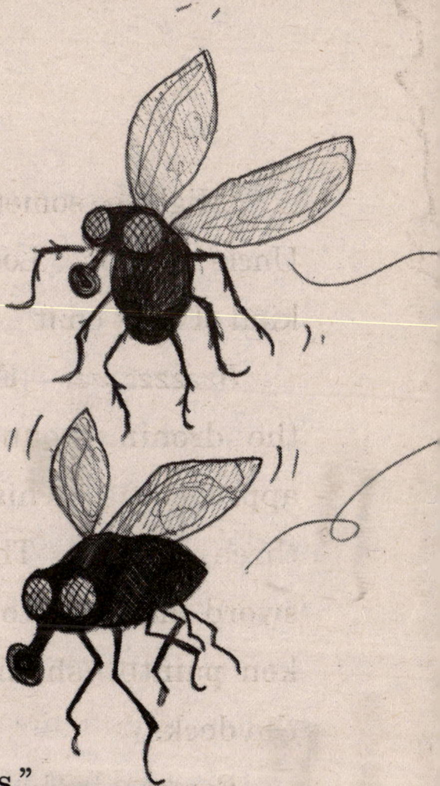

Uncle Noggin rolled up a corner of torn newspaper and waved it in the air. "Go on, off you go. Buzz around somewhere else, you 'orrible lumps."

"I think they're after our food supplies," said Button.

"No chance," cried Lily. "We'll fight to the end!"

Behind them, Mr. Dregby had dropped

to the outer edge of his web. He couldn't resist the look of the juicy flies and mini buccaneer snacks.

He dropped again, bouncing toward Button on his strong, silky thread.

"Look out behind you!" screamed Lily, but it was too late. Quick as a flash, Mr. Dregby wrapped his creepy, hairy feelers around Button's head and started doing his best to pull him up into the web.

Lily grabbed hold of Button around the middle, followed swiftly (well, when I say swiftly . . . errr . . . not really) by Old Uncle Noggin, who grabbed on to Lily by the coattails. So now there was a tug of war, with Mr. Dregby on one side

and Button in between, as Lily and Uncle Noggin held tight, refusing to let go.

Captain Crabsticks had finished fighting off the flies. Fearlessly, he climbed on to the top of a cotton spool to wave his darning needle at the huge spider.

"Get those blasted hairy pins of yours away from our cabin boy, you filthy arachnid."

The more the crew pulled at Button, the tighter Mr. Dregby's grip became around his neck. He was struggling to breathe and the spiky hairs from the spider's huge legs scratched his face.

Close up, the spider's eyes whizzed

and twirled in every direction and its mouth was opening wide.

"Take that, you . . . you . . . eight-legged monkey," the Captain shouted, and at that moment he managed to stick the needle into one of the spider's legs. Mr. Dregby made a strange spidery *squuueeeeaaaal*, let go of Button, and went shooting back up his thread into the corner.

"That'll teach him to mess with the might of the miniature pirates!" said the Captain. "Retreat to the deck, crew."

Lily and Uncle Noggin dragged Button to his feet and they all hurried inside the bottle. Then, for the second time that day, they pulled the cork tight into the neck.

Mr. Dregby stared at them, six angry eyes and bared teeth glinting at them through the glass.

"That was too close for comfort," said Lily, her heart beating fast.

"Well done," cheered Old Uncle Noggin. "We deserve a tasty snack for that."

"How long do we have to keep this up for?" said Button, sweating after his ordeal. "It's exhausting."

"And it's red hot today," said Uncle Noggin, wiping his brow with his handkerchief.

The flies bashed against the bottle, buzzing and hovering. Mr. Dregby walked over the glass ceiling, wrapping his silk

backward and forward around the bottle.

"We're being taken over," said Button.

"Something has to be done, and soon," agreed the Captain. "No one and nothing bullies the inch-high pirate crew and gets away with it."

The Crow & the Pitcher

All that heat inside the bottle was making the place feel like a greenhouse. Normally they'd keep their food in the ship, but they'd had to put it in an old matchbox on the shelf to stop it from spoiling. And when Button ventured out to fetch supplies he discovered something.

"Garghhhh! The flies have eaten the grub."

"WHAT?" cried Uncle Noggin. "ALL of it?"

"Every last morsel," said Button, hanging his head and pulling his wet hair back over his face. "Except the cheese. They've gotten sick on the cheese."

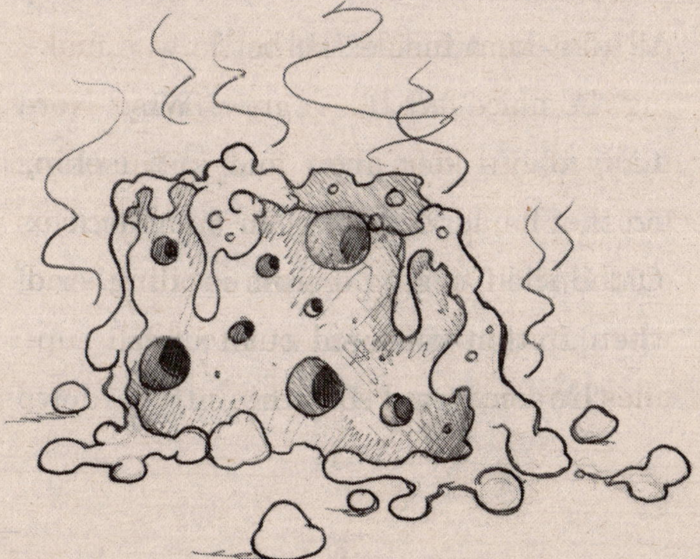

"Urrrrrghh, the nerve of it," gasped Uncle Noggin. "I was looking forward to grape juice and cheddar tonight."

"We're stuck in here, it's red hot, I'm bored, AND I'm thirsty," said Lily, frowning.

"How about a good old story, then?" suggested Uncle Noggin. He *always* had a story, and now was no exception. "It'll help to take our minds off things."

"A story? What . . . now? Why?" said Lily, folding her arms and still looking cross. She settled into her hammock as Old Uncle Noggin perched on a timber of the ship that stuck out at an angle.

"Go on," said Button, sitting down

alongside them. "It will take our minds off the mayhem."

"Well, you reminded me, being thirsty an' all that, about the story of a clever old crow. It's an ancient story, mind you. But it's a good 'un."

"Okay," said Lily, "I'm all ears."

"Well, it was a hot afternoon in the middle of a blisterin' summer when a crow swooped down to see if he could find water to drink. There didn't seem to be a drop *anywhere*. Not until he found a shady corner of a garden and an old jug that had collected rainwater from a thick nest of old vine leaves.

"But the jug was only half full and try

as he might, the crow just couldn't reach far enough to take a drink. Not even with his long beak."

"What did he do, what did he do?" urged Button.

"Well, he took hold of a pebble in his beak and dropped it into the water."

"Why?" asked Button.

"Listen," said Lily, "and you'll find out."

"Then another and another, until slowly he could see that the water was beginning to rise upward.

"He kept on going, one pebble after another. Hard work it was too, for an old crow. Backward and forward in the heat and it was starting to feel to the crow like it wasn't worth it after a while.

"But when eventually the water came to the top, he took a good long drink and then flew off up into the blue sky, feeling happy and satisfied."

"Ahh, that's clever," said Button.

"Of course," said Uncle Noggin. "Mr. Crow's a wise old bird."

"That was very good, Uncle Noggin.

Thank you. But it hasn't helped our situation. AND it's made me more thirsty," said Lily.

But Button thought he might know what the story really meant. They had to be wise, just like the crow.

First things first. They would need a late-night trip to try to get some supplies. A good climb in the dark down to the old desk, where they knew there was dried pasta in the drawer with the broken keyhole.

Pasta was light and easy to carry. Then they'd draw off some hot water from the leaky pipe and soak it until it became soft. Not the best meal, but at least it would stop them feeling hungry.

Button pattered over to the wrist-watch that was fastened to the wall. It was late. Mr. Tooey would be snoring away upstairs by now and more importantly, the dog would be fast asleep. It was a good time to leave. He was looking forward to it: a short breathing space, away from the shelf. A bit of adventure, maybe a touch of danger. Or at least some peace and quiet away from Uncle Noggin.

"I think you're right," said Lily. "Let's take our time. As long as we keep an eye out for Old Hairy Legs, it should be fun."

When darkness came, Button and Lily set off together, leaving the Captain and Uncle Noggin to look after the ship.

It was cooler now that the light had dropped. A silvery-blue moon lit the way, and for a moment it felt almost magical along the shelf.

As they skirted around the plant pot, something made a sound.

"What was that?" hissed Button.

"What?" whispered Lily.

"It was a . . . strange sound. Like a *shhquelch* but not just a *shhhquelch*. More like a *thump* but not just a *thump*. Kind of both. A kind of . . ."

"You mean a *shhhquellllump*?" said Lily.

"Yes, *exactly*," said Button. "You heard it too, right? What was it?"

"No, I didn't hear it. No idea!" said Lily. They carried on with their mission and the *shhhquellllump* was soon forgotten.

Climbing down to the desk was an easy task for Lily and Button, especially when they were alone. In no time at all they were rooting around in the drawer with the broken keyhole.

"This one will do," said Button, after they had spent some time searching through the rubble. He was dusting off a piece of macaroni. They had no idea why the dried pasta sat among the paper clips and staples, but it was useful. Lily found one too, and with an old shoelace and a safety pin they started hauling their meal back to the shelf.

Climbing over the odds and ends, Button noticed a book on plants. He couldn't resist investigating the pages in the blue moonlight.

"What are you doing?" whispered Lily back to him.

"I just thought . . . I might . . ." (Every time he found a picture or an interesting paragraph he went silent, studied it, and carried on again.) ". . . be able to see . . ."

"Be able to see *what*?"

"AHA . . . there it is!" he said, stopping at a picture of a plant that looked identical to the one Mr. Tooey had brought to the shelf.

"Oh . . ." said Button, "Look . . . it's a V E N U S F L Y T R A P."

"What's a veenos flytrap?"

"V E N U S," said Button. "It's . . . oh my goodness, it says here it's carnivorous! Catches its prey in a trap, triggered by tiny hairs."

Button heaved hard on the book's cover with both hands and slammed it

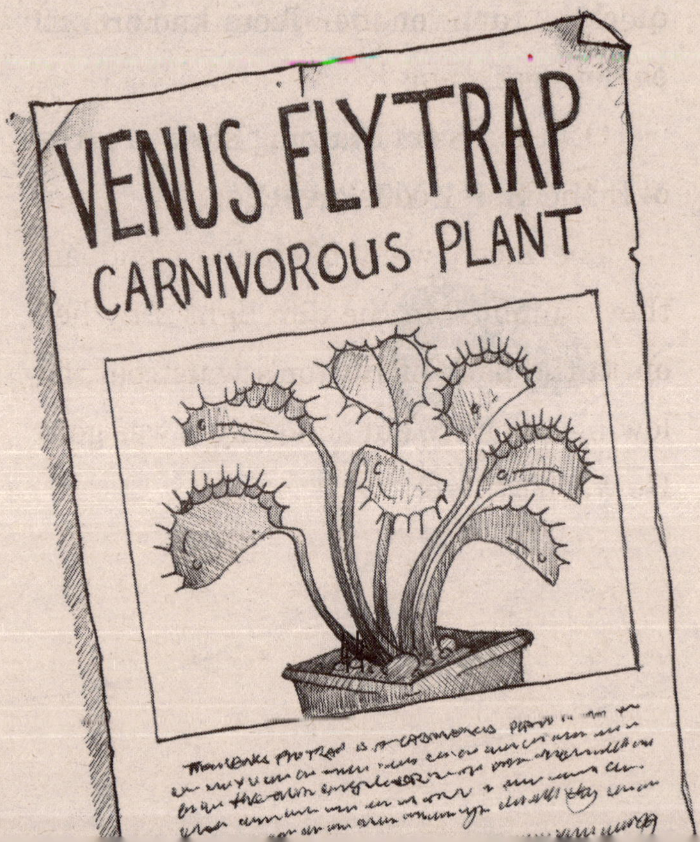

shut. “Lily, we need to warn the Captain and Uncle Noggin.”

“Why? What does ‘car . . . ni . . . vorous’ mean?”

“It means it eats living creatures,” said Button. “If that thing gets hold of any of us, we’ll be plant food. We need to be quick . . . and let the others know. Come on, let’s get going.”

Off they went, making slow progress over the messy odds and ends.

The moon went behind a cloud and they stumbled in the dim light. Lily held on to the back of Button’s waistcoat, following carefully, but suddenly it was gone. He wasn’t there!

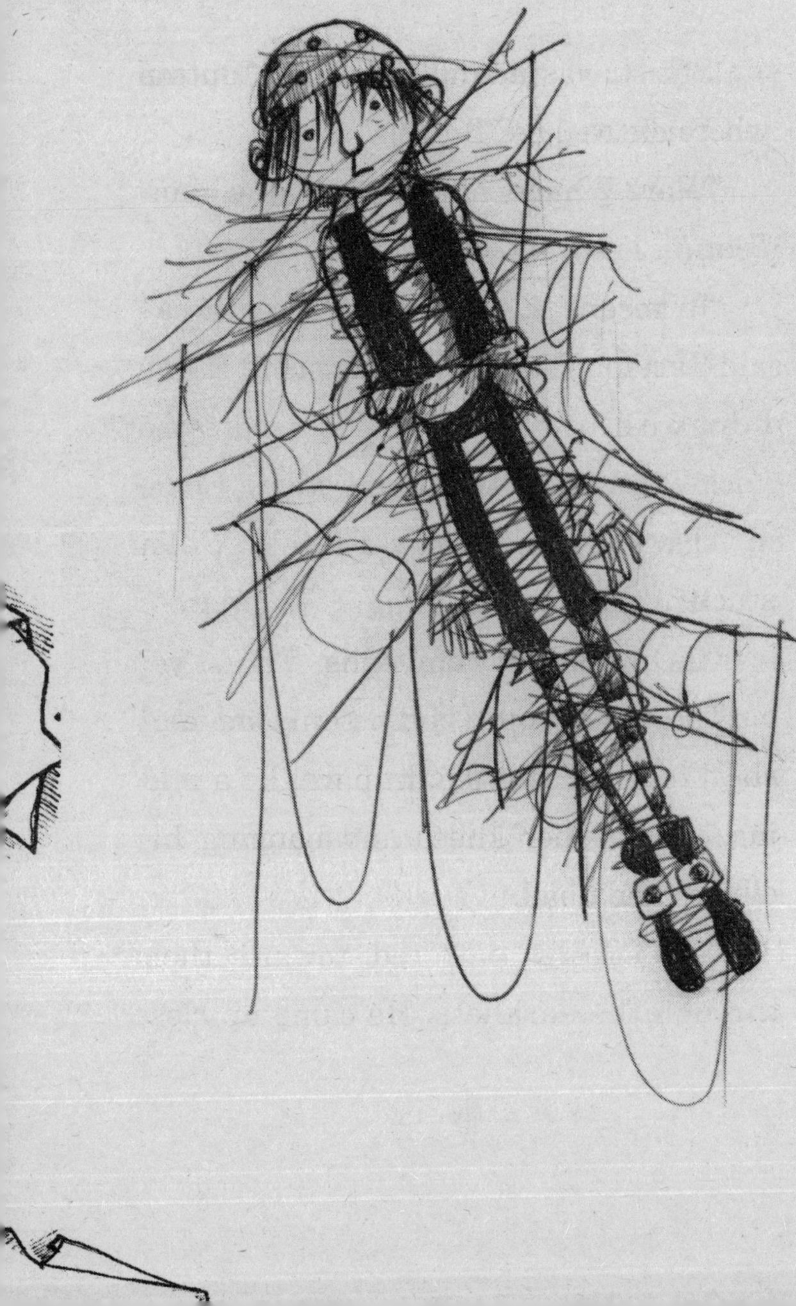

She stood still and called out. “Button, where did you go? Button?”

“Here,” came his voice in the dark. “I think I’m trapped.”

“Where?”

“Don’t come near,” he insisted. “It’s . . . I think it’s . . .”

“What?”

“It’s silky and sticky. I think . . . I’m stuck in the web.”

“NO,” said Lily, panicking. “I’ll get you out!” But she slipped and within a moment she’d fallen inside the deep well of a milk jug, grazing her knees and banging her elbows and head.

Mr. Dregby pattered toward them through the darkness. He came up close to Button, his six eyes looking him up and down.

"Well, well, well . . . how exciting!" He circled Button, wrapping him up in more silky thread. "One served up on a plate . . . and one in the cupboard for later," he chuckled, peering into the jug. "What a fine menu. For the moment I shall return to my corner and sleep off my last meal. Don't go away now. I shall look forward to having you for dinner tomorrow. Good night, children. Sleep well."

"Hmmmm. I wonder why those second-rate shipmates still haven't got back," said the Captain. "I'm presuming they haven't been squished or eaten."

"Perhaps we should go and check," suggested Uncle Noggin. "You never know what's around at this time of night."

"Well, I guess a stroll along the shelf won't hurt. Let's see what we can see, shall we?"

Uncle Noggin got himself up out of his favorite piece of sponge, and Captain Crabsticks sprang to his feet. Jones lifted his head, meowed, and went back to sleep.

"That's right, old chap, you keep an eye on the camp," said the Captain. "We won't be long. Back in a whisker." He stroked Jones's head and tickled his chin, making him purr loudly.

Only Button's face could be seen sticking out from the coiled-up, silky sleeping bag that he was now trapped in. He couldn't see Lily in the bottom of the jug and she couldn't see him stuck in the webbing. But they could hear each other.

"Try not to shout out or move," said Lily. "You'll vibrate the web and it'll bring Mr. Dregby back down. We should try to escape while he sleeps."

"Good thinking," said Button. "But how?"

"I'm not sure yet. I'm thinking."

"Me too."

The silhouettes of Uncle Noggin and the Captain wandered along in the darkness. A quick stroll along the shelf had revealed nothing. It was still and silent. Something wasn't right.

"I say, old Noggin, how about we climb up on to that greenery and take a look out from the top there?" suggested the Captain.

Uncle Noggin was none too keen on climbing. "Oh I don't know, Cap'n, my back isn't what it used to be you know and . . ." But before he could protest any further he was already lagging behind.

Button heard the voices coming closer. The familiar sound of his captain for sure, and the puffing and panting and complaining of Uncle Noggin.

"Come on, old chap, keep up," said the Captain, climbing the side of the pot like a monkey.

Lily could hear them too. She had to make them hear her, even from inside the jug. She bellowed a loud "*HELP!*" and it echoed around her.

"Well, shiver me seashells," said the Captain. "I think I can hear a cry for help."

"Can't hear nothing!" replied Uncle Noggin, who was now pulling himself up

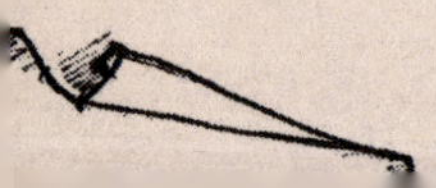

on to a huge spiky green flower. "Let me climb a bit higher."

"HEEEEELP!"

"Ah, there it goes. It's young Lily." He turned toward the shout. "Don't worry, we'll be there in no time, old girl," called the Captain. "Where the devil are you?"

"Milk jug!"

"Don't go near the plant," said Button, but he couldn't shout because he knew he'd vibrate the web.

"Can't hear you, old chap. Be there in a minute. Just as soon I've reached the top of this plant."

"Arghhh, NOOOO!" shouted Lily, but by now her crewmates were climbing over the green tendrils and standing on the flower heads. “Get away from it, it’s—”

“Ah there you are, Button old chap. Fear not, we’ll have you out of there in no ti—” *SHHHHQUELLLLUMP!*

“Well that’s strange,” said Old Uncle Noggin, “one minute the Captain was right there in front of me and the next minute he was g—” *SHHHHQUELLLLUMP!*

Suddenly it was silent. The sounds of Uncle Noggin and Captain Crabsticks rambling on and tugging themselves along to make a rescue had stopped completely.

“Oh dear,” squeaked Button quietly from his cocoon. “Lily, I know where the *shhhhquellllump* came from.”

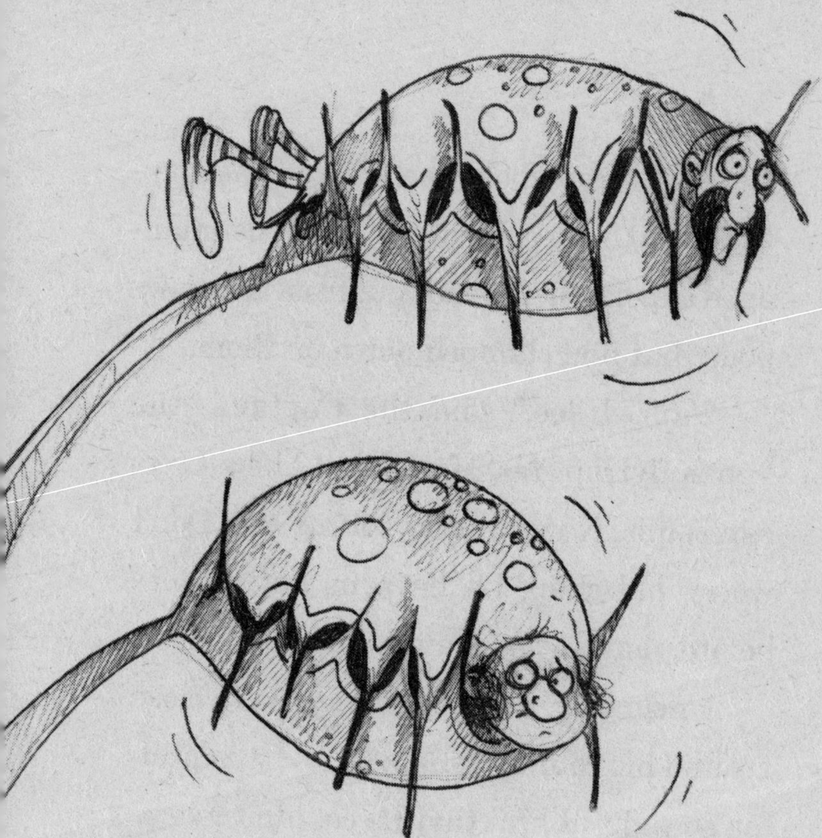

“Where?”

“From the flytrap. When it . . . you know . . . *catches* . . . something.”

As Button spoke, he spotted the Captain and Uncle Noggin, who had just managed to poke their heads out from the spiky pods that had clamped down on them.

"Ahh, I see," said the Captain, "the Venus flytrap. Yes, of course, I knew I recognised it. Now . . . errr, let me see. Don't worry, old chap, I'll have us out of here before you can say Davy Jones' Locker."

Uncle Noggin's trap struggled to close around his rounded shape, but it was pulling so tight at him that he couldn't move.

Button's face stuck out of his silk sleeping bag. Lily sat helpless in the bottom of the jug. And the two old sea dogs lay wrapped up in their spiky coats with

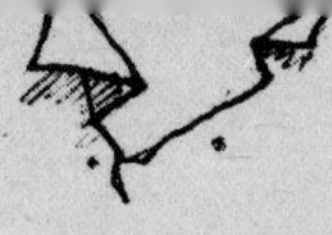

their heads peeping out at the tops.

“What now, Captain?” said Button. “Any ideas?”

“Errrum . . . bear with me, old chap . . . I’m thinking.”

They waited in darkness and silence and not one of them could imagine what they should do next.

Mr. Dregby opened his eyes. His prize was still waiting. *Not long before breakfast*. He smiled. And then he went back to sleep.

The night moved on. Outside the shop window the stars shone and an owl hooted in the distance. Everyone lay trapped in their junk-shop prisons, growing tired but knowing that time was not on their side. If they went to sleep it would be disastrous. They might not ever wake up again!

The Captain and Uncle Noggin tried hard to wriggle free. They pushed and pulled with their arms and legs, but it seemed that the more they struggled inside the spiky pods, the tighter they closed around them.

"Best keep as still as possible, Old Noggin. Looks like we're in for a tricky evening."

For a moment Lily thought she had a solution. "If I can rock the bottom of the milk jug, I can tip it right over and climb out," she said, explaining her plan to Button as she began to put her brainstorm into action. It was a simple idea but it could work. If she could break free she could cut the others down from their traps. She ran from side to side, banging her hands on the rounded walls at each end until she felt the base lifting slightly from the floor. The jug gradually began to rock on its base until it was swaying.

"Keep going!" said Button. "It's working, it's moving. If you get out of there you can free us all!" He was beginning to shout loudly in excitement. The spider stirred in his sleep.

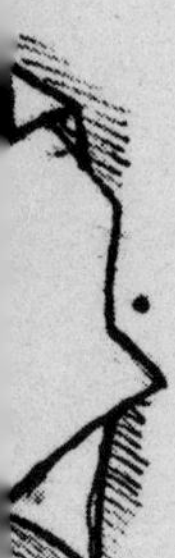

The jug rocked from side to side, the movements getting bigger until eventually . . . *CRASH*. It overbalanced, and with it went a stack of bits and pieces that had been piled up next to it. Match-

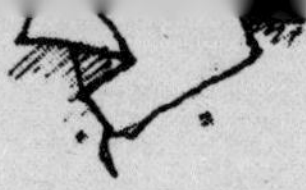

boxes and pepper shakers. Paper clips and drawing pins. Some dice, a pine cone, and a pile of old coins spilled across the shelf, and a cotton spool went rolling off the edge.

The jug had tipped over, but not all the way. The mustard-jar bathtub had

stopped it. Lily still couldn't climb out.

"Ah drat," said Lily, puffing and panting, "I'm worn out." She sat to catch her breath. "All that effort for nothing."

"Do you mind?" said Old Uncle Noggin. "I'm trying to die in peace."

Just then a strange tunnel of light appeared in the room. It was Mr. Tooey. He had heard the noise and came peering over at them with a flashlight. The glare was blinding and they stayed still, panic-stricken as the searchlight seemed to peer right into their faces.

"More pests," he muttered. "Where are you?" And he ran the flashlight's beam along the shelf.

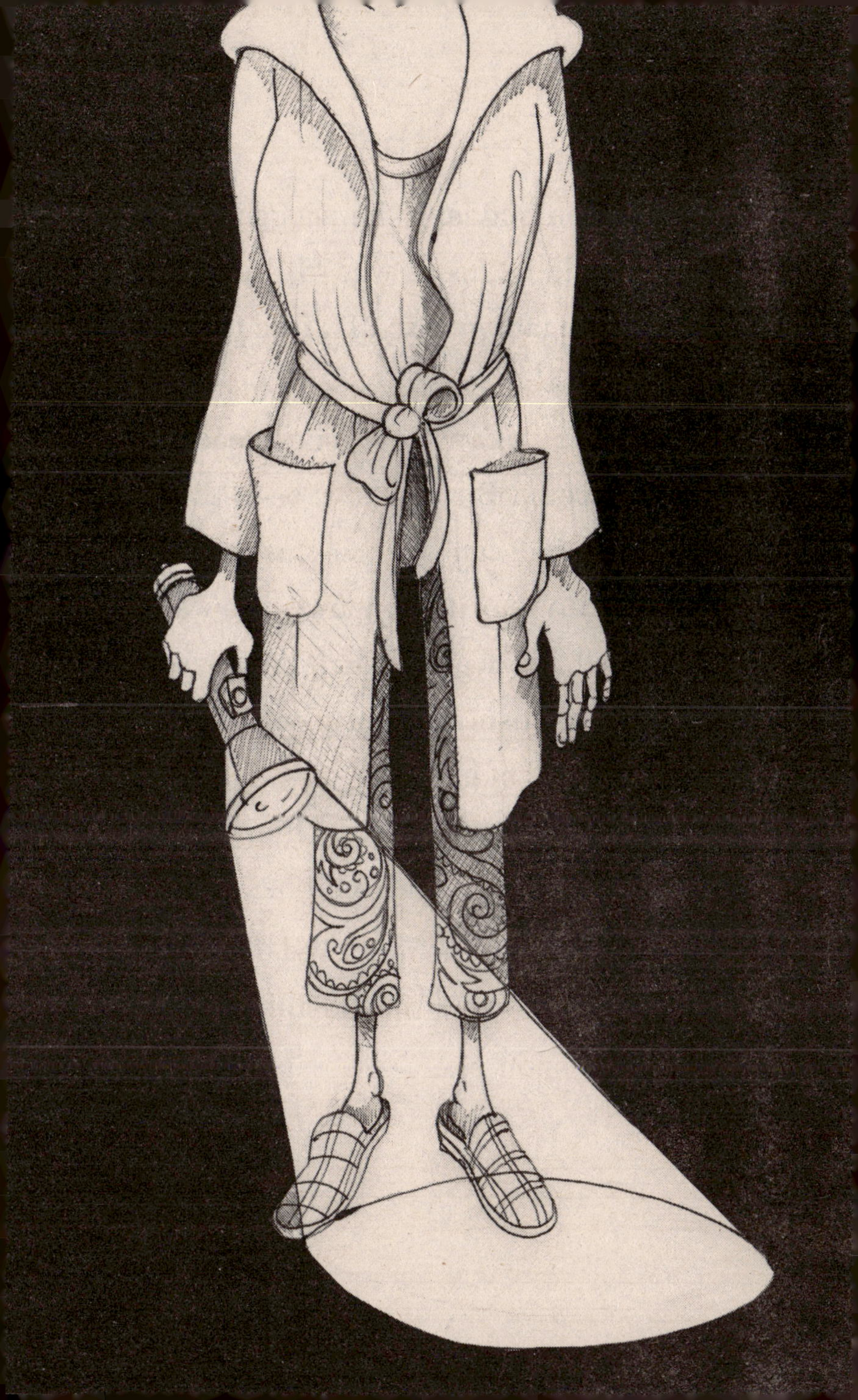

And then suddenly he was gone and all that could be heard was, "If I ever get hold of those mangy mice, I'll feed them to the alley cats."

"Phew, it's okay. He's gone. Good try, Lily," whispered Button. "I've been thinking. Maybe if I can stretch this web far enough, I can tear it away from the wall." He pressed his feet against the plaster and began to push. He kept going until he was on the tips of his toes.

The web stretched around him. He felt the silk straining and he could hear bits of thread springing and snapping. It took all his strength. He could feel his legs grow-

ing weak but he kept on pushing. He was almost there.

But the web was too strong and when it had gone as far as it would go, it sprang back and flattened him against the wall with a *thud*, keeping a tight hold on him.

Eight legs pattered down the silk and six narrowed eyes glared at him. "Now, now, Button. You're testing my patience. All your fidgeting is keeping me awake."

Mr. Dregby pulled a length of Button's emergency shoelace from his backpack and with his pincers he shredded it to pieces. Button watched the sharp jaws effortlessly cut into the rope.

"The more you annoy me, the angrier I get. Do you understand, Button?"

Then Mr. Dregby wrapped him up tighter with his silvery thread and returned to his corner.

Button gulped and felt his heart thumping hard in his chest. A bead of sweat ran down his forehead.

"You know how long a spider ACTUALLY keeps its victims in its web, don't you, Button?" said Uncle Noggin.

"Yes, I do, and I don't wish to remind myself, thank you."

"Just thought it might inspire you to escape," shrugged the old pirate.

"Sure," Button answered. "Want to

know how a Venus flytrap eats its prey? Holds on to it tight and slowly digests every inch of it by releasing a nasty chemical and dissolving its victim."

"Oh . . . well, yes, I knew that, Button. Thank you. In fact, I think I can feel it happening right now."

"There'll be nothing left of us," cried Lily from the milk jug. "You'll be plant food, and Button and I will be spider breakfast. The Pocket Pirates will be extinct."

"Nonsense," said the Captain, "I'll have us out of here in no time."

He looked around, racking his brain, and realizing there wasn't much he could do with his body gripped tight from the head downward.

"Errrum . . . but if I don't," he continued, "then I've had a thought . . ."

"What is it?" said Button.

"Well, we can't leave the ship without a captain. Someone needs to look after her."

"And . . . ?"

"So, if we're no longer here . . . I hereby declare Jones will be captain of the ship . . . just in case!"

"Pah, charming," laughed Button. "I'm trapped in the web of a giant spider. There's no real hope of escaping and I'm

likely to be breakfast in only a matter of hours. And if by any miracle I manage to escape, my Captain is going to be a soggy, old gray kitty."

No one answered. Button was exhausted. They *all* were. It had been a long day. Button felt himself drifting, his eyes closing. The silk cocoon, fastened tight around his body, was somehow comfortable. He tried to fight the urge, but he was helpless and eventually he drifted off into sleep.

An Unexpected Meal

BZzzzzZZZzzzzzZZZZzzzzzzz.

The very thing that had woken Button the previous morning suddenly roused him again. But this time he was glad of it. He turned his head, his eyes staring into darkness. He felt a tightness around him and quickly remembered that the comfortable feel of his hammock had been replaced with silky spider thread and that he was in great danger.

"Wake up," said Button, whispering carefully over to the Captain. But it was no good. The Captain couldn't hear him, and Button dared not wake the terrible Mr. Dregby by shouting too loud.

Fortunately for the Captain, the fly buzzed over to him and landed on his face, shocking him into opening his eyes. His cry of surprise woke Uncle Noggin, who until now had been drooling over the side of the spiky plant.

Old Noggin went into a sudden panic.

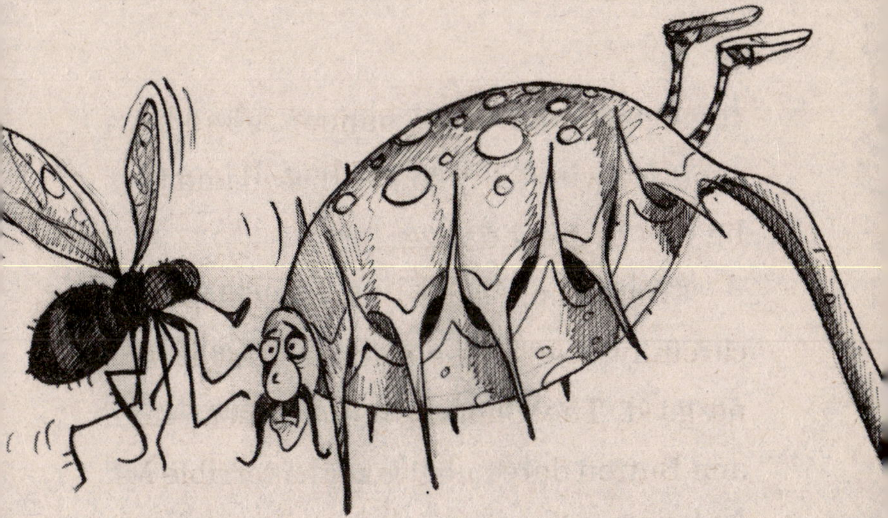

"I can't feel my legs! Arrrgghhhhhhh! It's eaten half of me already!"

"Shhhhhhhhh," said Lily from thc milk jug.

"Calm down, you old walrus. You're all there, I can see from here," said the Captain. "I've

been dreaming about spiders. Must have been that book I was reading. Interesting creature, the common house spider. He's a recycler . . . a bit like us, I suppose. Eats his web so that he can spin one again if he doesn't get too much food in the meantime."

"Clever idea. Isn't nature amazing! Not much of a meal though," said Uncle Noggin, distracted by the talk of food.

"Oh I don't know! Tastier than Button, I expect," said the Captain, chuckling.

"Oh very funny," huffed Button. "This is no time for jokes. We need to think fast."

"I'm trying," said the Captain.

"No you're not, you're half asleep." And then Button had a thought. "What was that bit again?" he asked. "The bit about eating its web."

"Well, apparently the web is made from protein, so instead of wasting it, he can gobble it up it and then produce more spider silk."

"Ah, I see. You mean a bit like packing up your tent and moving on to another campsite," came a voice from the jug.

"Very good, old girl," said the Captain. "Exactly like that."

Button didn't say anything else. He didn't need to. He took a glance above him to check that Mr. Dregby was still asleep. In the distance he could see some hairy legs sticking out from the web. They were still.

11

It was early, but a faint light was starting to come through the window. *This will work,* he said to himself. *I know it will.*

He began to tear at the web with his teeth. After all, they were the only thing he could use. But it was obvious: He would eat his way out, just like the spider eats his web.

Button was tearing out great chunks, but it wasn't pleasant. It stuck to his face like cotton candy, and tasted like a mouthful of belly button lint. He spat it out below, and soon he had freed the tight coil around his neck. Leaning over toward

his shoulders, he chewed away until they were free too.

He went slowly, so that the web didn't vibrate, but it didn't take long before he

was easing his body out at the top, freeing his hands. Then he was pulling and tearing at the thread around his legs, and he knew that he was almost ready to make the leap.

Stretching his fingertips as far as he could, Button reached the edge of the nearby mirror frame, and pulling himself toward it, felt his feet come out of his shoes, leaving them behind. He was free!

The Captain and Uncle Noggin had been watching Button's every move.

They kept still and silent. If they made a fuss now the old eight-legged beast would appear and it would all go wrong again. They waited and watched in wonder at the antics of the lad who they knew was the best cabin boy in the world.

Button climbed across the mirror frame, using his

hands and feet to hang on, and when he had gone as far as he needed, he dropped on to the shelf.

"Right," he said, rubbing his hands. "Time for the tiniest of the mini pirate crew to show how brave he really is."

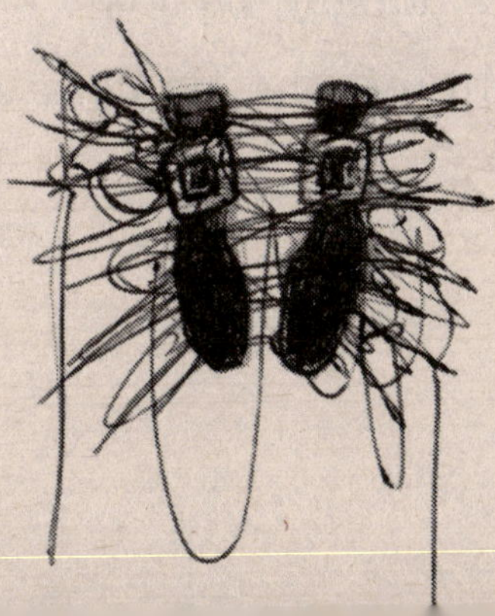

Button Bites Back

Button went over to the plant pot and stood beneath the Venus flytrap.

"Don't worry," he called. "I'll have you chaps out of there in no time. But Lily comes first. If that eight-legged beast wakes up and decides he's hungry, he'll see I'm gone and drop straight into the jug for his breakfast."

"But what if we get eaten by the plant?" said Uncle Noggin.

"Don't worry, it takes days," Button reassured him. "Did I not mention that? I read it in a book."

"But what if Dregby decides he likes the look of US? We're trapped and helpless."

"He won't come anywhere near this plant," said the Captain bravely. "These things don't just eat flies, they eat anything. Spiders, bugs . . . oh, and small pirates of course."

"What are you going to do, Button?" asked Uncle Noggin.

"You'll see," whispered Button. He ran

to perch on a pile of old books, level with the top of the milk jug. Lily's familiar face was staring up at him out of the dark.

"Have you out of there in no time, old girl," said Button, pulling his emergency rope from his backpack. And then he was reminded that now it had been shredded it was nowhere near as long as it needed to be.

"Ah drat. Suffering seashells," said Button. "Now what do I do?" He knew he needed to be extra careful not to fall into that jug or they'd both be a free meal and that would be the end of everybody.

Whatever his alternative plan was, it needed to be foolproof. He looked around, but couldn't see anything that would

work. There was a pencil, but it wasn't long enough. There had been a cotton spool, but Button had watched it roll off the shelf when the jug crashed into the corner. And the other spools lying around were empty—the thread had already been used for various adventures.

He stood on the books, scratched his chin, and leaned against the water pipe.

And then, in a moment, it came to him. "Of course!" he whispered, a smile breaking across his face.

"What is it?" said Lily, "*What?* What do you mean, '*Of course!*'?"

"The story, Lily. You know: the crow and the jug."

"I need more of a clue than that!"

"You'll need to swim," said Button, pointing to the water pipe. "Look, this is where we take the cork out to fill the bath," he said, pointing to where the little stopper had been forced into the leak so that when they wanted to take a bath in the mustard jar, they could fill it with water.

The jug had crashed into the corner and was in just the right position. Button pulled on the cork and the lukewarm water started dribbling out.

"It's a bit like your story," Button pointed out to Old Uncle Noggin, "except the other way round. I'm pouring water into the jug until Lily rises to the top!

Then, when she's out, we'll get you both down."

"You're a clever old stick, aren't you, Button?" said the Captain proudly.

"My feet are getting wet," said Lily. The water was filling her boots and there was nothing she could do but stand in it and wait for it to rise.

The jug was filling nicely, but the light from the window was growing brighter. Dawn was on the way.

"Keep going, you're doing a marvelous job," said the Captain.

"Yes . . . hurry up!" said Uncle Noggin. "I think my feet are being eaten alive."

"Uncle Noggin, even the grubbiest

plant on earth wouldn't be interested in your feet," laughed Button.

"Don't worry, you're safe," called Lily from below as the water reached her neck.

The water was swirling around her now. She had to keep kicking her feet to stay upright and she could feel herself starting to float up inside the jug.

"It's working, Button. It's working!"

But up above in the corner, something could hear Lily's voice. It opened its eyes. There were six of them.

At first Mr. Dregby was sleepy. But then he remembered about his breakfast, and he was excited.

He came out of his corner, stretching his legs and bouncing along his thread toward the place where Button had been. But when he got there, the bundle was empty, torn to shreds. What in the world had happened to the juicy young prize he had captured? Nothing had ever escaped from his web before.

Mr. Dregby's eyes turned red. He

grumbled and grimaced with his sharp teeth. His prickly hairs stood on end. Off he went to search: Surely Button wasn't

far away. But there were so many crevices and hiding places to be checked.

Button had climbed back to the shelf, to think about how to rescue his other shipmates as soon as Lily was free.

"I'm almost there!" called Lily. But as she reached for the edge of the jug, the six eyes that were looming back at her did not belong to Button.

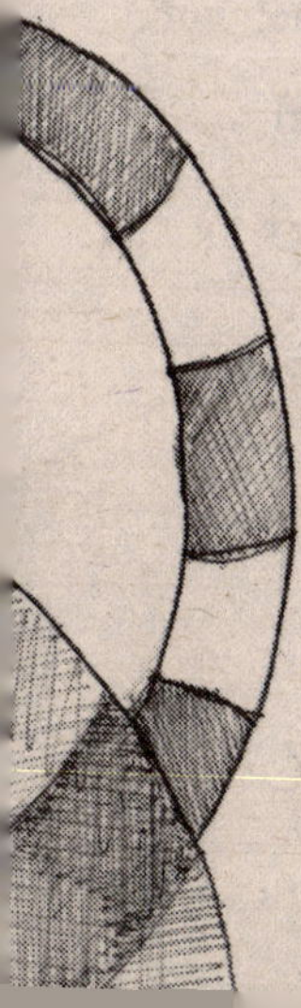

A Brush with the Enemy

Captain Crabsticks had drifted off to sleep again, wrapped in his spiky green sleeping bag. Uncle Noggin was awake, worrying about being eaten alive, trying to distract himself with thoughts of food. At that moment he was imagining a crisp, full-size cornflake.

If Button had looked he would have seen Uncle Noggin chewing an imaginary mouthful, but he was too busy formulating the escape plan to take any notice of Uncle Noggin's nonsense.

He climbed the books again, hoping

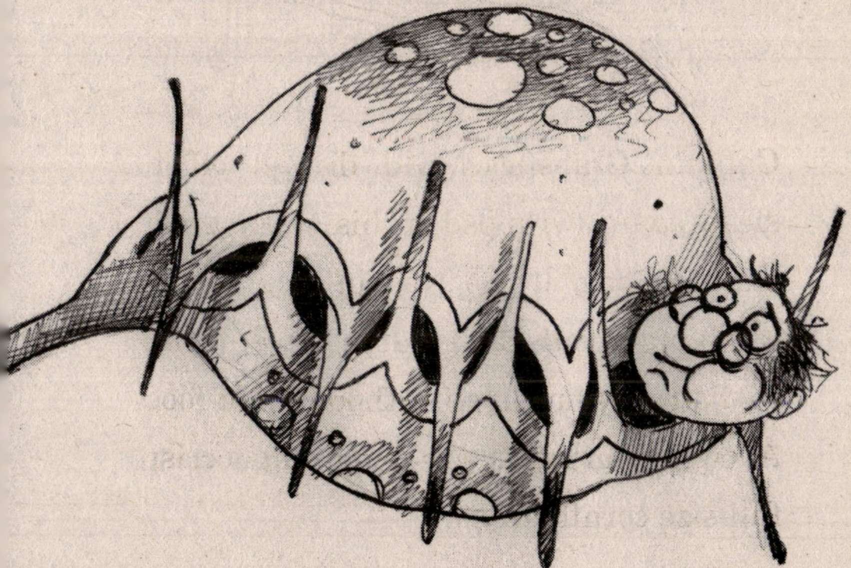

that Lily would be floating high enough to be pulled out, but when he got there something was in the way. He couldn't quite make it out at first: a dark shape looming over the edge of the jug.

"Dregby!"

Lily was gasping and panicking in the water. She flapped her arms and kicked her legs. Above her, hairy legs hung down. Large teeth were frighteningly close to her face.

"Well, well, well," said the spider. "What good news. I *will* be getting my breakfast after all."

He dropped a little lower. Close up, his eyes were even meaner.

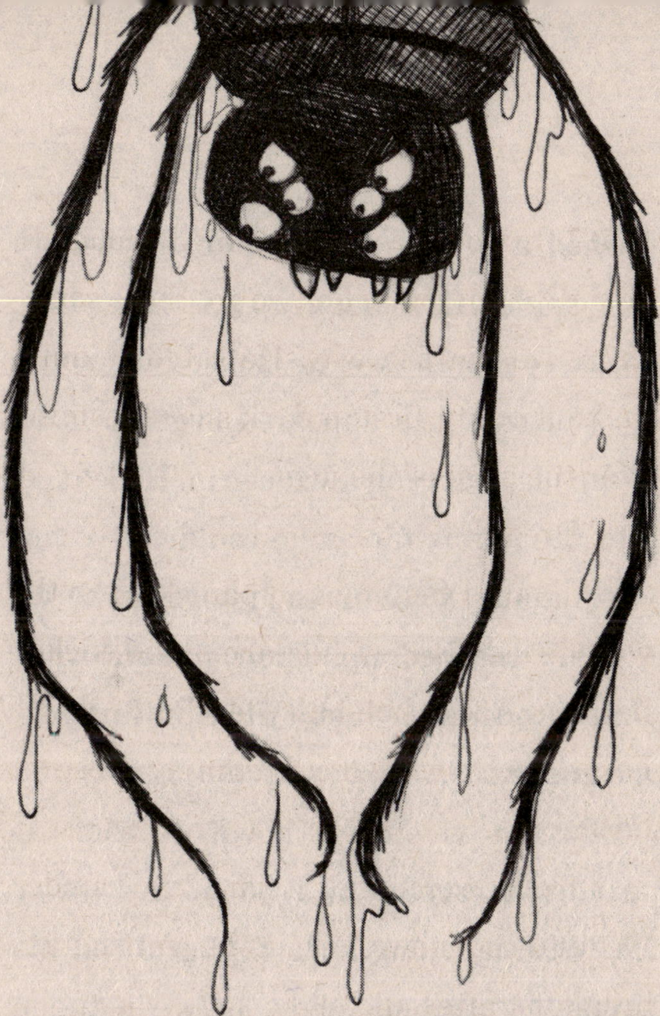

But just as she let out a yelp, a huge splash soaked Mr. Dregby. Button had pushed a pepper shaker into the water! The spider flew back up his thread in shock, so sopping wet he looked ridiculous.

Button's face appeared over the side of the jug, grinning a wide grin. He leaned into the jug as far as he could. "Give me your hands, Lil. I can reach you from here."

Lily reached up. Their fingers were almost touching. "Just a little bit further," she gasped.

Button stretched down further. If he wasn't careful he'd be in the water too! With a strong kick, Lily grabbed his hands . . . and somehow, between them, they managed to ease her over the rim of the jug and out on to the pile of books.

Mr. Dregby was as angry as he was soaking wet. His breakfast, lunch, and dinner plans had been foiled. "Those pesky miniature pirates have escaped my clutches once again," he moaned as he dried his hairy legs. "Flies for breakfast. I've had enough of those little buzz balls to last me a lifetime. And their noise is keeping me awake at night."

Lily and Button tumbled quickly down the books and up to the shelf. All the commotion had woken Captain Crabsticks again, and Uncle Noggin had been distracted from his dream about cornflakes.

"I'm drenched!" said Lily. "But glad to be alive, thanks to you." She perched on a rusty teaspoon, shivering.

Button scratched his head and looked at the flytrap.

"Get me first," said Uncle Noggin. "I can't feel my body. I think there's only my head left."

"I doubt if it could have eaten that much, old chap," said the Captain from his perch.

Lily was looking around for something they might use to pry open the jaws of the hungry green monster. There it was! In the corner, covered in dust and stringy, broken bits of cobweb. An old cocktail stirrer.

She darted over to it and leaned it against the wall, stamping on it until it snapped in half.

"This is perfect," Button said, as she handed one half of it to him.

Just then Mr. Dregby dropped down right in front of Button's face. His eyes were all agog; his teeth were showing. He was still dripping with water.

"Just tell me, Button. How did you get out of my trap? That's all I want to know."

"Stay away from me, Dregby," said Button, pointing the stirrer at him.

"Oh dear . . . you're shaking, Button. I thought you were a fearless pirate! Perhaps you're not so brave after all."

"Come any closer and you'll be on the end of this cocktail stirrer." Button gripped it harder and stood his ground.

"I haven't done with you yet, Button. Don't get too clever. You're only a weak cabin boy."

And then Mr. Dregby crawled back into his dark corner, while Button tried to stop his knees from trembling.

"Thank you, Button," said Lily, who was shaking with cold and a little bit of fright. "You're a hero."

Special Delivery

Button climbed on to Lily's shoulders, hoisting himself up into the bottom of the plant pot. As he landed in the soil, he realized he was still without his shoes. He took a look up at the web and could still see the buckles showing through the thread. How would he ever get them back?

"First things first," he said to himself. Maybe later, when they'd rescued the rest of the pirate crew.

"You're too late," cried Uncle Noggin. "There's barely anything left of me."

"Don't be silly," said Lily. "Calm yourself down. We'll have you out of there in a flash."

Button decided that he would get Uncle Noggin out first, because he

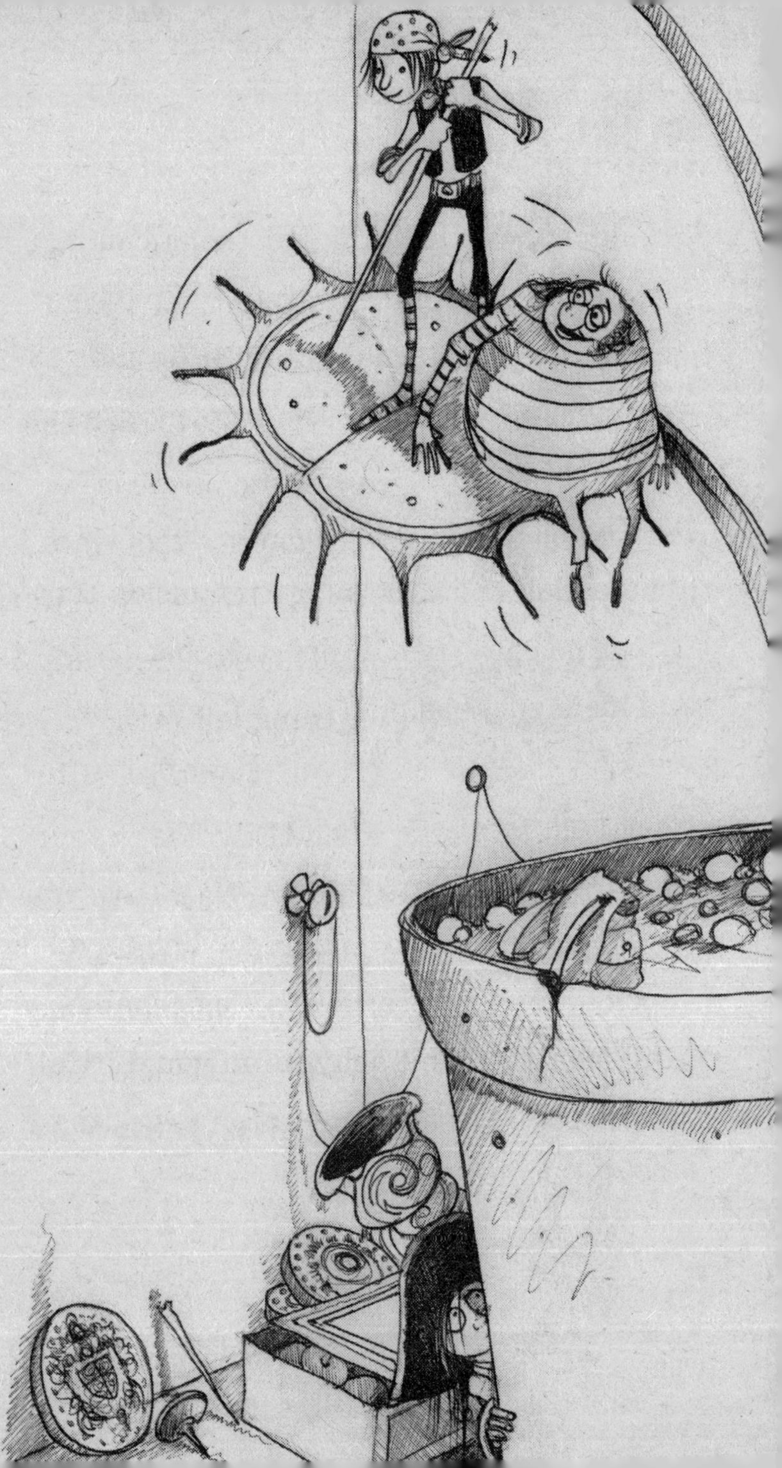

couldn't bear listening to the moaning any more. He climbed carefully up to the old pirate's pod, making sure he didn't get near any more of the hungry, green spiky mouths.

Reaching Uncle Noggin, he shoved one end of the cocktail stirrer inside the green pod and then he heaved it back with all his might, easing Uncle Noggin out bit by bit. As soon as he could move, Uncle Noggin couldn't get free fast enough. And when he did he yelled out loud.

"I'm alive!" he shouted. "I'm alive! Look, I'm all here! Arms, legs, hands, and feet. Little bit achy, mind you. Little bit sore. These bones aren't getting any younger, you know, Button."

Lily helped Old Noggin down from the pot and then climbed up the plant herself.

"Well done, old girl. Now if you don't mind, I wouldn't mind getting out of here myself," pointed out the Captain. And so, with Lily's help, Button pulled him out from the deadly pod.

"You're a bit gooey!" said Button. "You'll probably need a bath."

Both the Captain and Uncle Noggin were covered in a sticky, slimy, green mess, and there was a slightly odd smell coming from them.

"Well, at least it will scare the flies off," laughed Lily as she climbed back down, avoiding the pods.

At last, they all gathered on the shelf. The older ones covered in green goo, Lily soaking wet and frozen, and Button without his shoes. None of them had managed a night's sleep, and they were still extremely hungry.

Jones came running up to them and brushed against Button's legs.

"Ah there you are Jones, old boy. Well

done for playing captain while we were trapped. You did a marvelous job. Extra fish for you tonight."

"So much has happened I can't remember what we were trying to do before all this started," sighed Lily.

"Well, we were trying to fight off the flies, and they'd taken all our food, and old Dregby was getting far too close. . . ." said Button.

"Ah, that's right," said the Captain. "Now—"

Just then the Captain was interrupted by a delivery. Something bundled in thread came dangling by a single strand of silk above their heads. Slowly it came down until it was in midair in front of Button's face.

They looked up to see Dregby on the ceiling, lowering the parcel like some kind of spooky, eight-legged postman. "Special delivery for your cabin boy, Captain."

Button took the parcel in his hands. It was his shoes! He could see the gold buckles through the silvery thread. He tried to tear the webbing open but it was wrapped too tightly, so he bit into it, tearing with his teeth.

The shoes were in there all right, just as he'd left them. It wasn't a trick.

"Why did you do that?" called Button, looking up at the spider.

"Why did I do *what*?" came the voice from above.

"Give me my shoes back? Why would you do that?"

"I wanted to see how you got out of my trap," said Mr. Dregby. "And now that I know you used your teeth, next time I'll wrap that mouth shut so you can't bite your way out. I'll get you in the end, Button."

And then he was gone again, through his silvery silk doorway and into his corner.

“Don’t worry, Button. He won’t ever get you. Not a chance,” said Lily.

Button was cross. “Hmmm, we never got a chance to deal with that web, did we?” he muttered to himself. “I’ve got a plan. I need a shoelace from the sea chest, and a cotton spool. A darning needle and some grease. I’ll show that spider not to mess with the Pocket Pirates.”

Perfect Plans & Sausages.

No one knew quite what Button had in mind, but they went along with it because when Button had a plan, it usually worked like clockwork. The shipmates watched him hook up the cotton spool to the shoelace and hold it in place with the darning needle. Then he fastened it to the old music box.

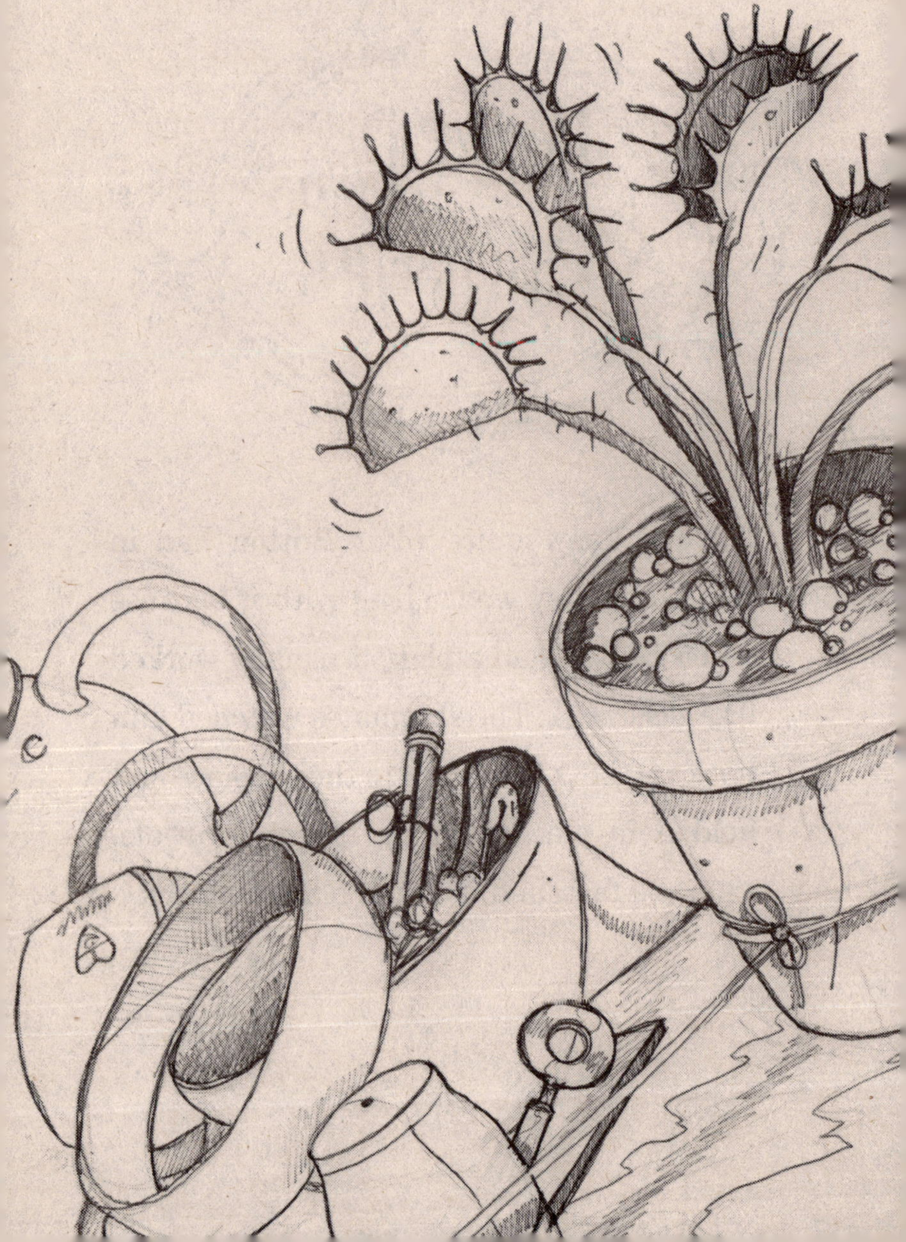

And only when they saw him haul the shoelace around the plant pot did they see what he was doing. He smeared the grease along the shelf from the plant pot toward the corner.

"Uncle Noggin, I want you to use your strength to wind the lever as far as it will go on the music box."

"Aye aye, cabin boy," nodded Uncle Noggin. He hobbled along the shelf to the music box, and he and the Captain leaned against it as he turned the lever until it was fully wound. The music started to play, the barrel turned and pulled the shoelace until, in turn, it pulled the plant pot along the shelf. Lily and Button helped it along with a good, old shove from behind and, gliding over the grease, it sailed smoothly into place under Dregby's web.

"Jolly good work, Button old boy," said the Captain.

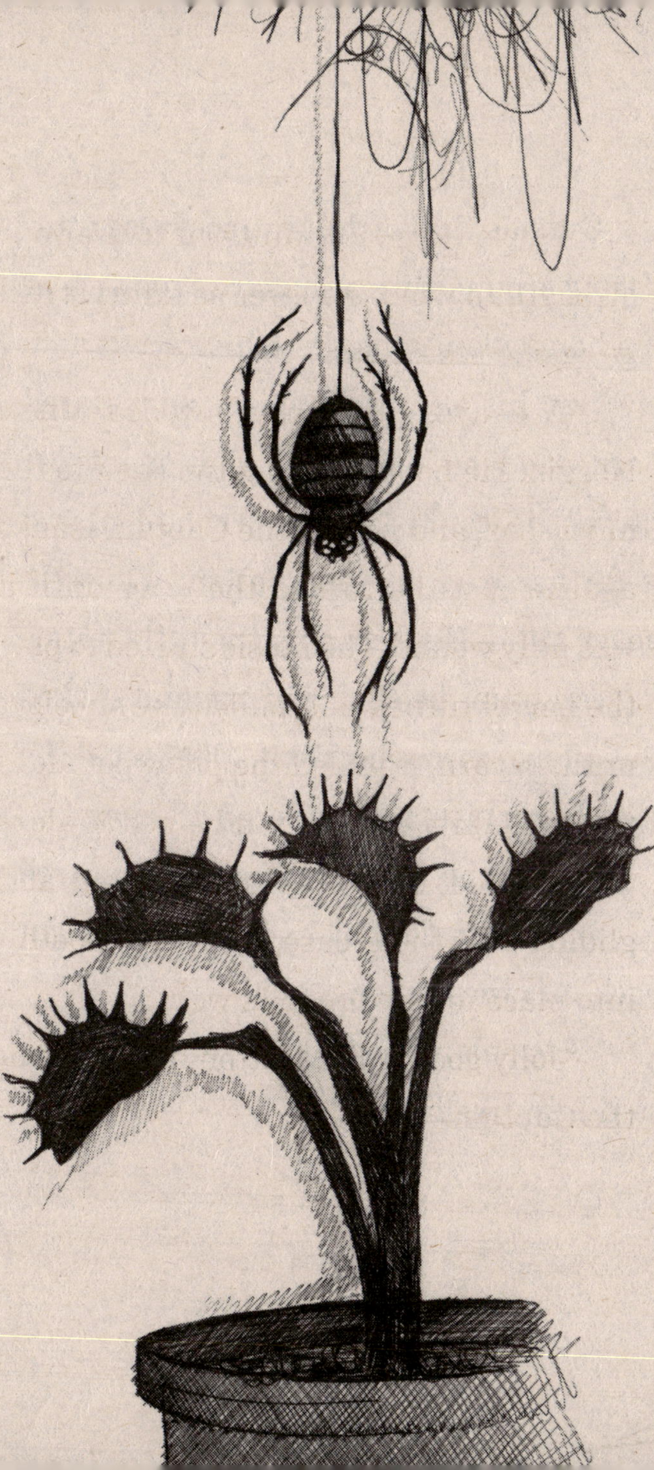

Outside the bottle, Mr. Tooey was wandering around with a sausage sandwich in his hand when something distracted him. He put his sandwich down and stared hard. Had he really put that plant pot there? He could have sworn he'd placed it farther over, in the sunlight. Oh well, never mind. He picked up the little watering can from the shop window and soaked the plant through. Then, distracted by something else, he wandered off again.

When the Pocket Pirates ventured out again, Mr. Dregby had retreated right back into the corner.

"Your plan worked a treat, Button," said Lily. "Well done."

"Good work," said Uncle Noggin. "Dregby's packed up his tent and moved along."

"Now listen here. Open your ears, buccaneers. Did someone order takeout?" said the Captain.

"Not much chance of that!" groaned Lily.

"Stop teasing," said Uncle Noggin. "I'm considering eating some dusty old cobweb at the moment."

"If I don't eat soon, I'll be ill," said Button.

"Well, there's a huge sandwich at the end of the shelf, so if I were you I'd get moving. Tally-ho!" shouted the Captain. "Let's get what we can!"

Was it true? Was there really a sandwich at the end of the shelf? Perhaps it was an illusion, brought on by lack of food.

"Oh my goodness," whispered Button. "I think it's . . . sausage."

"SAUSAGE!" yelled the crew. "ATTACKKKKK!"

The pirate crew raced toward the gigantic meat feast. Together they moved like a well-oiled machine, removing huge lengths of meat, scooping up the butter, pulling off chunks of bread, and munching as they went along.

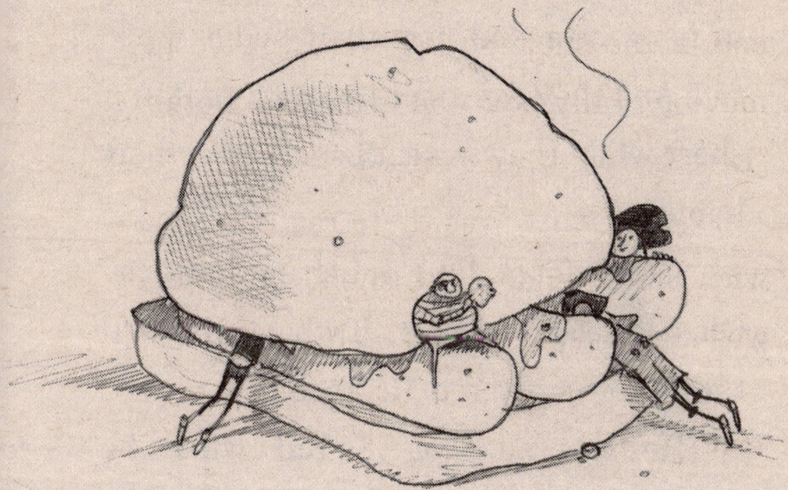

There was nothing like the surprise of food being delivered to the door. It hadn't happened often, but Mr. Tooey couldn't have chosen a better time.

They retreated below deck and ate and drank until they were almost bursting.

All was good. Mr. Dregby was back in his corner and now their bellies were full. And they were so exhausted that in a short while they were all snoring in their hammocks.

"Now where did I put that sandwich? Oh, of course, on the shelf when I watered the plant," muttered Mr. Tooey.

He was sure of it. But when he returned to the main part of the shop, he couldn't believe his eyes. Where his sandwich had been were just a few crusts, and what looked like tiny footprints in a smudge of ketchup.

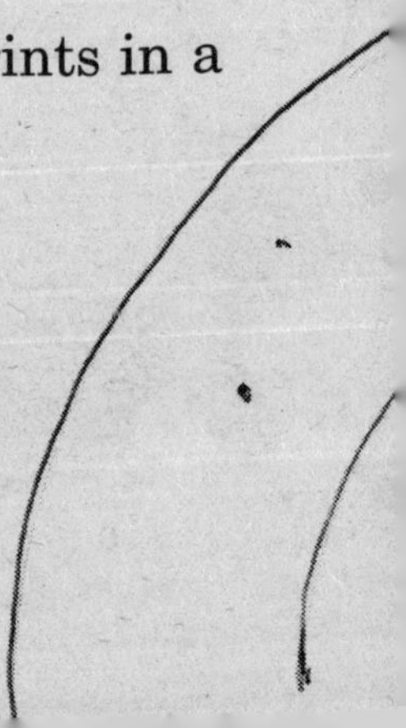

"Not again. I must be dreaming," he groaned.

But of course he would never say anything about it. People would think him mad. Wouldn't they?

Doyle's basket
HALLWAY
BACK DOOR
REAR HALLWAY
STORE ROOM
HALL
SITTING ROOM
Mice
BOOK SHELF

The place called Fridge (here be treasure)
The broken plug
KITCHEN
The Ship in the Bottle
SHOP
SHOP
12
SHOP WINDOW
FRONT DOOR
N
W
E
S
The Old JUNKSHOP

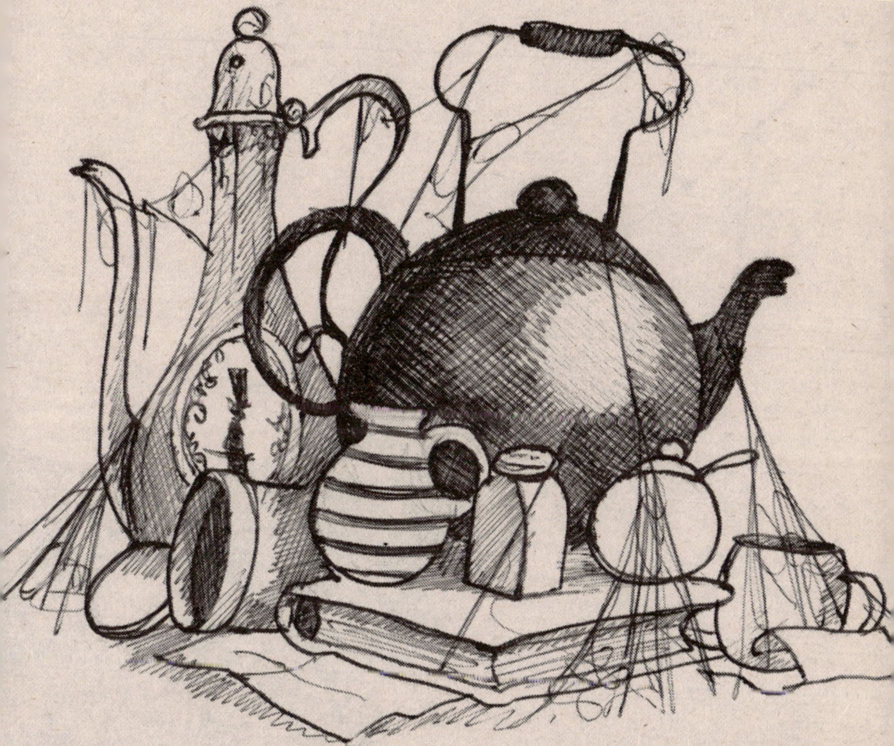

Les ateliers bijoux
Mes bijoux phosphos cosmiques
Qui brillent dans le noir !
DEUX COQS D'OR

La créatrice des bijoux

Roxane Guéguen est une jeune créatrice, graphiste et illustratrice normande. Après des études dans le graphisme et un stage en tant que graphiste dans l'édition, elle a décidé de vivre de sa passion créative en créant son entreprise : **Sunrise Studio.**
Passionnée par les loisirs créatifs depuis toujours, collaborer avec Deux Coqs d'Or était comme une évidence.
C'est avec beaucoup de plaisir qu'elle a imaginé et conçu ces bijoux cosmiques !

Sommaire